To my sweet granddaughter Sydney.

With love always, Grandma

—C.R.

For my mom.

—R.K.

Text copyright © 2017 by Carol Roth
Illustrations copyright © 2017 by Rashin
First published in the United States, Great Britain, Canada, Australia,
and New Zealand in 2017 by NorthSouth Books, Inc., an imprint of
NordSüd Verlag AG, CH-8005 Zürich, Switzerland.

First published in the United States, Great Britain, Canada, Australia, and New Zealand in 2017
by NorthSouth Books, Inc., an imprint of NordSüd Verlag AG, CH-8005 Zürich, Switzerland.

Distributed in the United States by NorthSouth Books, Inc., New York 10016.
Library of Congress Cataloging-in-Publication Data is available.
ISBN: 978-0-7358-4274-8 (trade edition)
1 3 5 7 9 • 10 8 6 4 2
Printed in Poland by Drukarnia Interak Sp. z o.o, Czarnków, October 2016
www.northsouth.com

Hold Your Temper, Tiger!

By Carol Roth • Illustrated by Rashin

North South

Little Tiger had a temper. Sometimes he got angry if he didn't get his way.

"Bath time, Tiger! Make sure you wash your tail."

"Not now!" he grumbled.

He would yell . . .

or cry . . .

or stomp his feet.

Sometimes he did them all.
"No more cookies, Tiger!"

"**MORE!**" he yelled, stomped, and cried.

One day Mama asked him to clean up his toys.
Tiger didn't want to.

He got angry.
"NO!" he said.

Mama didn't like that.
"Don't make me ask you again," she said.

The more she asked him, the angrier he became.
"I'M NOT DOING IT!" he said.
Mama made an angry face and said, "You had
better hold your temper, Tiger, . . . or else!"

UH-OH!

Little Tiger didn't know what "or else" meant.
He didn't want to find out.

Maybe it meant no playtime.
Maybe it meant no books.

Maybe it meant . . . **NO DESSERT!!!**

Perhaps I *should* hold my temper, Little Tiger thought.
But what does that mean?
And where should I hold it?

Should I hold it in my pocket?
Should I hold it in my hand?

Should I hold it in my underwear?

Then Little Tiger had an idea.
"I know just where to put it!" he said.

He took a deep breath.
He gathered up all his anger from deep down inside.
And then he let it out.

"R-O-A-R-R-R-R-R-R-R-R-R!"
went Little Tiger as he held his baseball cap over his mouth.

Then he put the cap on his head.
He put a smile on his face.
He quickly cleaned up his toys
and went down to dinner.

"That's better," said his mother as she
gave him a hug.

"You know I don't like it when you lose
your temper," she said.

"Oh, don't worry," said Little Tiger. "I'll
never lose my temper again. I know exactly
where it is."

DATE DUE

JUL 5 1989	JAN 2 '93	MAR. 28 2005
JUL 24 1989	JUL 23 '94	AUG. 01 2005
AUG 09 1989	MAR 29 1997	AUG. 16 2005
AUG 26 1989	JUL 29 1998	NOV. 02 2005
SEP 23 1989	APR 24 2000	JUL 29 2006
OCT 16 1989	APR 09 2001	APR. 05 2007
OCT 28 1989	NOV 24 2001	JUN 26 2009
NOV 27 1991	JUN. 26 2003	AUG. 05 2010
JAN 13 1991	NOV. 04 2003	AUG 12 2010
MAY 4 1992	JAN. 07 2004	APR 09 2011
JUN 17 1992	MAR. 02 2004	
NOV 16 '92	NOV. 15 2004	DEC 08 2011

OCT 17 2012
E JAN 18 2013
JUL 10 2014
JUL 28 2015
JAN 18 2018

ANNIE & MOON

a story by
MIRIAM SMITH
illustrated by
LESLEY MOYES

Gareth Stevens Children's Books
Milwaukee

Library of Congress Cataloging-in-Publication Data

Smith, Miriam.
   Annie & Moon.

   Summary: Her little black cat Moon gives Annie
   feelings of security and affection during a series
   of moves with her mother.
   [1. Cats—Fiction. 2. Moving, Household—Fiction]
   I. Moyes, Lesley, ill. II. Title. III. Title: Annie and Moon.
   PZ7.S65635An   1988   [E]   88-42909
   ISBN 1-55532-928-4

North American edition first published in 1989 by

Gareth Stevens Children's Books
7317 West Green Tree Road
Milwaukee, Wisconsin 53223, USA

This US edition copyright © 1989
Text copyright © Miriam Smith, 1988
Illustrations copyright © Lesley Moyes, 1988
First published in New Zealand by Mallinson Rendel Publishers Ltd.

1 2 3 4 5 6 7 8 9 94 93 92 91 90 89

15035

ANNIE and Moon are good friends.
They even look alike, which is strange,
because Annie is a girl
and Moon is a cat.
Annie has black hair
and green eyes like Moon,
and Moon has black fur
and green eyes like Annie.

ANNIE and Moon have not always lived together.
When Annie was little,
she lived with her mother and her father
in their own little house in the country.
But when she was four, her father went away
to live somewhere else,
and the house seemed empty without him.
"It's lonely here," said Annie's mother, Meg.
"Let's move into town,
where there are more people."
So Meg sold the little house,
and she and Annie packed up their clothes
and their furniture
and went to live in an apartment in town.

THE apartment was just two rooms
on the top floor of a large building.
There were no other children in the building
and Annie had no one to play with.
So one day, Meg brought home a tiny black kitten.
"I think I'll call him Moon," said Annie,
"because he's as black as a black, black night
with no moon."

AT first Moon was very unhappy
away from his cat family.
He walked around and around,
calling for his mother.
He didn't like his new home.
Annie stroked him.
"Poor little cat," she said.
"It isn't easy for a little cat
to get used to a new home."
Annie lined Moon's basket with sheepskin
and put it in the corner of the kitchen.
Moon seemed to like that,
and after a while he settled down.

BUT it cost a lot of money to live in an apartment.
"We haven't got enough money to live here," said Meg.
"Let's go and live with Auntie Maire."
So Meg and Annie packed up their clothes
and their furniture
and moved to Auntie Maire's house.

AT Auntie Maire's house,
there were lots of children to play with.
But . . .
"Cats aren't allowed to sleep inside," said Auntie Maire.
So Moon had to sleep out in the shed.
Annie cried when Moon was put outside at night.
Moon cried too.

MEG had some friends who all lived together
in a big old house.
"There's room for you both," they said,
"and we don't mind if cats sleep inside."
So Meg and Annie packed up their clothes
and their furniture
and moved to the big old house.

A baby in the big old house pulled Moon's tail,
and squeezed him hard.
Annie put Moon's basket in her room
where he would feel safe.
Meg was often busy with her friends,
so Annie talked to Moon.
"Poor little cat," she said.
"It isn't easy for a little cat
to get used to a new home."

THEN Annie's grandpa died.
"I wish you would both come and live with me,"
said Grandma. "I would like the company."
"Should we go?" asked Meg.
"Yes, I like Grandma," said Annie.
So they packed up their clothes
and their furniture
and went to live with Grandma.

GRANDMA'S house was just right.
There was a garden with trees
for Annie and Moon to climb,
and Grandma and Annie had lots to talk about.
Moon seemed to like it too.

B<small>UT . . .</small>
Grandma had a dog named Brutus
who loved to chase cats.
Moon arched his back and his fur stood straight up
whenever Brutus came near him.
Annie put Moon's basket right under her bed
so he would feel really safe.

ONE day Brutus crept into the bedroom
when Moon was asleep.
There was a terrible fight!
Moon was so frightened
he jumped out of the window and ran away.

ANNIE called and called, but Moon didn't come.
When she went to bed, she left the window open for him.
That night Meg got into bed with Annie.
It seemed like such a long night.
They waited and waited.

JUST as the sun began to come up,
there was the sound of scratching outside the window,
then a thump on the bedroom floor.
Something landed on the bed and began to purr.

IT was Moon!
Annie sat up and hugged him.
Meg sat up and hugged them both.
"You don't know," said Annie, "how very hard it is
for a little cat to get used to a new home."
Meg smiled. "I do know," she said.
"It's hard for little girls too —
and for mothers."
Annie thought for a while.
"Let's stay here.
Brutus and Moon should get used to each other.
Then we can all get along."

AND do you know,
after a while,
they did get along just fine.